THIS BOOK BELONGS TO
T-REX

....

A is for Apple.

B is for Ball.

C is for Car.

D is for Dog.

E is for Egg.

F is for Fish.

G is for Guitar.

H is for Hat.

I is for Ice Cream.

J is for Jump Rope.

K is for Kite.

L is for Lemon.

M is for Moon.

N is for Nest.

O is for Orange.

P is for Pizza.

Q is for Quilt.

R is for Rainbow.

S is for Sun.

T is for Tyrannosaurus Rex.

U is for **Umbrella.**

is for Violin.

W is for Watermelon.

X is for Xylophone.

Y is for Yarn.

Z is for Zebra.

Made in the USA
Thornton, CO
02/02/24 04:17:34

0b8bc84c-eddc-45cf-95a0-11df5dfc3656R01